Journey
to Another Star
and Other Stories

The Lerner Science Fiction Library
Roger Elwood, Editor

Journey
to Another Star
and Other Stories

Foreword by Isaac Asimov
Illustrations by Kathleen Groenjes

 Lerner Publications Company
Minneapolis

Published simultaneously in Canada by
J. M. Dent & Sons Ltd., Don Mills, Ontario

Manufactured in the United States of America

International Standard Book Number: 0-8225-0957-1
Library of Congress Catalog Card Number: 73-21478

Contents

Foreword

Science fiction is about change. It is written because there *is* change in our world. In fact, all history is the story of how human life has changed, from the discovery of fire to the landing on the moon.

In ancient times, change was slow — so slow that no single person could see it taking place in his own lifetime. Changes did not often affect the lives of ordinary people. Kings came and went, armies won and lost, but life went on as usual.

When the age of modern science began, however, the rate of change increased, and people began to take notice. By the time the steam engine was invented toward the end of the 1700s, changes seemed to be taking place every day. Suddenly, there were steamships and railroads and telegraphs and sewing machines. The lives of ordinary people were no longer the same as the lives of their parents and grandparents.

Naturally, people began to wonder what further changes in living their children and grandchildren might experience. To satisfy their curiosity, they turned to science fiction. Science fiction writers speculated about the ways that life might change in the future. They invented new and different societies and told stories about them.

In the last few decades, change has become so rapid that our civilization and our very lives depend on our being able to understand and control change. It is as though we were in a racing automobile that we had to learn to steer in order to avoid a crash.

Science fiction can help us gain control of our future. It can help us understand the importance of change and the nature of the changes that may soon take place. In this way, science fiction gets us used to thinking in terms of the future. Because it is the only form of literature that does this, it plays a very important role in today's world.

Young people who grow up with science fiction have a real advantage. The training in imagination and forethought that they receive makes them better able to solve the problems we face now, and the still greater problems that we will face in coming years.

New York, New York
April, 1974   ISAAC ASIMOV

George Zebrowski

Journey to Another Star

Looking back, 35-year-old Jack Kimball recalled the time when the dream of space travel had almost died. He remembered how the wind had whistled through the empty rocket towers, making them creak. One day, he had thought, the steel skeletons would topple over and be covered by the soft earth, like the bones of prehistoric dinosaurs. He recalled the hot Florida sun and the cool Atlantic breezes. Yes, he remembered it all, until at last . . .

. . . Jack Kimball was a boy again, and it was summer. Along with two other boys, he was standing in front of a wire gate. It was the closed gate to what had been the first spaceport in North America.

"Come on, Jack, there's nothing to do here," Frankie said to him.

The concrete road leading into Cape Canaveral was cracked in many places, and the painted letters of the keep-out sign were half peeled off. In another year or so, the abandoned spaceport was to be covered over with high-rise apartment buildings. Jack knew that unless something were done soon, the dream of space exploration would die forever.

"Come on," Frankie repeated. "Let's get going."

Ignoring him, Jack turned to look through the gate across the lonely flatlands of the cape. In the distance, a flock of birds rose from the ground, filling the sky with the sound of wings and crying. Once, powerful rockets had shaken the ground here, boosting spaceships up into the heavens. But all that had come to an end years ago, after the failure of the Mars project in 1987. Now, Cape Canaveral was just a ghost of its former self.

"Jack, we can't go in there," whined Craig, the youngest of the three boys. "It looks scary. My dad says there are big holes in the ground."

"Yeah, let's go back," demanded Frankie. "There's nothing to do here."

Jack could see that both of the boys were frightened, and this angered him. "You're just a couple of sissies," he said. He turned from them and began to climb the towering fence. When he reached the top, the other boys started to follow him. Jack had known that they would do this, but he would have kept going even if they hadn't.

He climbed halfway down the other side of the fence and jumped to the ground. Then he began walking toward the old rocket assembly building, a quarter of a mile away. The two other boys finished climbing the fence and followed far behind him.

As Jack walked, he wondered why there were no more rockets. Why was this place empty? Why had something so exciting been given up? Why did so many people do so many boring things all their lives when there were so many great things that remained to be done?

The immense rocket building rose more than 500 feet above him. His father had called it the Vehicle Assembly Building. He had said that because it was more than 800 feet long and 600 feet wide, the mammoth box could have had its own weather system inside—rain and all. In the old days, before the building was shut down, they used enormous fans to blow the air around so that rain clouds could not form inside. Jack wondered what the weather was like inside the big box now.

"Wait!" Frankie shouted. Jack turned and waited for the two boys to catch up with him.

"It's so big," Craig said. He was staring up at the building so hard that Jack thought he would fall over backward.

"What do you think it's like inside?" Frankie asked.

"It might be raining," answered Jack.

Frankie laughed. "You're crazy. How could it be raining inside? We're not dumb enough to believe that."

"I don't really know how," Jack answered, "but my father says it's true."

"Your father's crazy, too," Frankie said, laughing again. "Go ahead and prove it. Get inside and show me."

"I don't know how to get in."

"See, just like I said—there's nothing to do here. Let's go home, Craig."

"What's that tower over there?" Craig asked. He pointed to a huge tower atop a giant platform.

"That's the old launch-pad tower," Jack replied. "The whole side of this building would open to let in the standing spaceship so that a lot of guys could work on it inside to get it ready."

"Oh," Craig said.

"You're making it all up," Frankie said. "He's just trying to act big, Craig. Come on, let's get out of here."

"I'm not making it up!" Jack yelled, growing angry. "It's all true!" He held his hand over his eyes to keep out the noon sun.

Frankie laughed even louder this time. "Just because your father says so, huh? Boy, are you ever dumb."

Furious, Jack lunged at Frankie, knocking him down to the sandy ground. Then he rolled on top of him and pinned him down. "It's all true!" he repeated. "Say it!"

"Okay, I give," said Frankie.

"*Say it*! Say it's true!"

"All right, it's true. Now let me up."

Jack rolled off him and stood up. Moments later, Frankie jumped to his feet and started running back toward the gate, leaving little Craig behind. "It's NOT TRUE!" he shouted. "It's not!"

Jack did not shout back. He turned around and took Craig by the hand. "Let's walk around the assembly building," he said, "and I'll tell you all about it. Later, we'll go look at the launch tower. Okay?"

"Okay," Craig answered, smiling up at him . . .

. . . Hard to believe, he thought, but that had happened over 20 years ago. Now, as he sat in the control cabin of the first starship to Alpha Centauri, Jack Kimball was glad that the space program had not died. The development of the first real starship, 15 years ago, had brought the space program back to life. But something else had been needed—a new kind of engine that would enable men and women to reach the distant stars in months instead of years.

Jack had helped design that something else. He had studied physics in college and in the labs on the moon. He had grown up to be one of the first engineer-astronauts to test a warp-drive engine, and he had been chosen to pilot the first hyperspace ship to Alpha Centauri, the closest star to Earth next to the sun.

Although the bright multiple star was some 4.3 light-years away, Jack had crossed the space between the sun and Alpha Centauri in only two weeks—an incredible feat. When running at full force, the ship's engines could warp space fast enough to take Jack to any star within 30 light-years of Earth *in less than a year.* Interstellar colonization was thus a possible goal, provided that Earth-like planets could be found circling other stars. And Jack Kimball had helped make it all possible.

On his forward viewscreen, Jack now saw the beautiful three-star system that made up Alpha Centauri. While the two brightest stars—Alpha Centauri A and B—revolved around each other, the small red star called Proxima Centauri circled them. The sight was a diamond-jeweled dream set in a clear midnight of a million stars.

The ship was still too far out for him to see the system's only planet, but Jack knew it was there because he had helped detect it at the lunar observatory. He leaned forward and turned on the computer guide, which automatically sent the ship in the direction of the unexplored planet. About the size of Earth, the planet revolved around Alpha Centauri A, the largest of the three stars.

Once the ship had flashed beyond Proxima Centauri, the space between the two brighter stars grew larger and larger. Jack sat back in his seat and thought of all the time and energy that had gone into the space program. He recalled Sputnik I and Explorer I—the first artificial satellites; the Russian Vostoks, along with projects Mercury, Gemini, and Apollo—the first manned missions; and, finally, the doomed Mars project, which had ended with three Americans and two Russians dying on Mars when their landing craft crashed into the angry red planet. That catastrophe had almost ended the dream of space travel forever.

The two brilliant stars were now a terrifying sight on the forward screen. To Jack, they seemed to be giant atomic furnaces burning in the infinite cold of space. As he looked at them, he thought of all the unmanned probes that had been sent across space, faithful servants carrying out the plans of mankind, sending back knowledge until the day when man himself could follow. He saw himself again, years ago, looking through a telescope at Alpha Centauri, wondering what it would be like to voyage into that starry universe beyond the sun.

Now that he had reached that starry universe, Jack wondered what it would be like to look back at the sun and see it as only another star in the heavens. He pushed a button, and the screen showed him a view of the sun, a small point of light that he knew was home. He pushed the button again, and the view changed to show what lay ahead.

He had made it, he told himself. The planet circling Alpha Centauri A looked green and beautiful on the screen. He turned up the telescopic magnification and saw sunlight reflect from the blue ocean below. He saw the browns and greens of land, and the icy white of polar caps.

As he beheld the unexplored planet, astronaut Jack Kimball knew that he had remained true to the boy who had climbed over the fence and led the way to an abandoned spaceport. Yes, he was still that boy. Only now, 20 years later, he was piloting a starship several light-years away from Earth, leading the way to another star.

| Guidance

My father said it was time for me to have a robot of my own. "I think you're ready to take on the responsibility, David," he said. "Of course, you must understand that a personal robot is to be used, not abused. And the fact that I consider you ready for this step means that you must live up to it. If not, you can go on using the general family robot for a while. You and Mack seem to get along very nicely, and you might even be happier that way."

"Mack" is the name of the family robot who takes care of us when the personal robots are being serviced, or when they're outside doing things like landscaping. His full name isn't "Mack," but something a lot more complicated, which I can't even pronounce. I *do* get along well with him, but it's just not the same as having a robot of my own, like my mother and father do.

"No," I said to my father. "I really feel that I'm ready to have a robot of my own now. I'll take good care of it, I promise." (Now that I am 10 years old, I find that my father listens to me better than he used to.)

"Very well," my father said. "In that case, I'm going to give you Mack as your personal robot. We'll activate another robot from the stockpile for the general tasks."

"Give me Mack?" I said, trying not to sound too disappointed. "But I've had him for years!"

I like Mack, and always have. But I have to admit that when I used to dream about having a personal robot, I always hoped that it would be entirely new. Of course, I couldn't come right out and say this to my father; he's quite strict. And besides, he's been warning me for years that when the time came for a personal robot, I'd have mixed feelings about it.

"Maybe if I prove I can use Mack right," I said, "you'll decide I'm ready for a brand new one."

"Enough of that!" my father snapped. "We'll take this one step at a time, young man." He pressed his buzzer, alerting Mack to come into his study. (All our important discussions are held in my father's study. Now that robots take care of us and perform all the unimportant tasks, there's no need for fathers to work away from their homes any more.)

The door opened, and Mack wheeled himself in.

Somehow, I had always imagined that when this important time came, it would be an exciting and wonderful thing to look upon my own robot for the first time. But it was only Mack. He wasn't even shined for the occasion, and the faint noises coming from his mechanical limbs indicated that he was due to be serviced again.

"Hello, Mack," my father said. (He always talks to the robots kindly, and on a first-name basis. He says it's important to treat them as if they were humans.) "David and I have discussed things, and you're going to be his alone for a while, if it works out."

"That's fine," Mack said in his deep voice (which, come to think of it, sounds a lot like my father's voice). "I'll be happy to be David's alone."

"It's just on a trial basis," my father said, "and David knows that. If he shows himself incapable of taking on the responsibility for your servicing, or if he gives you any commands you find questionable, you'll come straight to me."

"Of course I will," Mack said. "But David and I have always gotten along with each other, haven't we, David? I'm sure everything will work out just fine."

"But that isn't fair!" I protested, watching Mack approach me in the quiet manner that personal

19

robots always approach their masters. "If Mack can go to you and complain any time he wants, then he's not really mine, is he? It's just as if he were on loan from you."

"Don't concern yourself with that," my father said in the voice he always uses when our talks are over. "*I'll* be the judge of who is loaning what to whom, and *you'll* kindly remember that you are only 10 years old!" He leaned toward some papers on his desk. "Now, if you don't mind," he said, "I'd like to get back to my work. I'm glad we've been able to work things out together, but I'm very busy, and I just can't spare any more time." He waved a finger at Mack. "Keep an eye on him, and see to it that he gets his homework done."

"Of course," Mack said, extending an arm toward me. "David and I will go down the hall right now and work on some spelling."

"It isn't spelling!" I yelled, heading toward the door, Mack right behind me. "I'm supposed to be studying *history* today. The history of robots—how they came to be built and to become our helpers—with special attention to the changes during the early 2000s."

"Of course," Mack said, taking my wrist. "Robots are forgetful sometimes, but I'll see to it that you get to your spelling. And there'll be *no fooling around*, young man! After all, I'm your personal helper now, and that should take a lot off your mind and enable you to study better."

"I know you'll do a good job, Mack," my father said, as Mack eased me down the hall.

"First," Mack said to me, "I'll help you finish your homework. Then, I'll help you get cleaned up for dinner. And after dinner, I'll draw your bath for an early bedtime. Now that I'm going to be your personal helper, you'll be able to do all the things you never had time for before—like studying, keeping clean, getting to bed early, and so on." Strange, but he seemed to pinch my elbow!

"I have a great deal of responsibility now," Mack continued. "It isn't going to be easy, you know." Suddenly, I felt *another pinch*, this one much harder than the first! "But since I'm going to be with you all day long," Mack concluded, "your parents won't have to worry about you so much." We continued down the hall, Mack behind me and pushing.

I just couldn't believe it! I felt *none* of the power and control that's supposed to go with having your own personal robot. But what could I do? Mack had a mind of his own, and my father was on his side.

"Hurry along now," Mack said.

"Yes, Mack," I replied. "Whatever you say."

Better
Dumb
Than Dead

Looking for her pet, 10-year-old Janet headed toward the open door to her uncle's laboratory. She was just in time to hear a thunderous crash.

"Floppy!" she gasped.

Floppy, her pet raccoon, was sitting atop a shelf laden with chemicals. He had accidentally knocked over a glass jar, sending it down among the test tubes and beakers on the table below.

"Now see what you've done!" Janet wailed. "Uncle Joel will be very upset when he sees the mess you've made. *Shame* on you!"

But the worst was yet to come. Panic stricken, Floppy scrambled down from the shelf and stepped into the pool of chemicals that had spilled from the broken glassware. Then he began licking the chemicals off his front paws.

"No, Floppy!" screeched Janet. "It might be poisonous!"

But Janet was too late. With tears in her eyes, she watched her pet lick off the last of the spilled chemicals. Then she held her breath and waited for him to double up in pain and die. But nothing happened; Floppy showed no signs of pain. Sighing with relief, Janet picked up the mischievous raccoon and cuddled him.

"Janet! What happened?" a voice boomed. And there, standing in the doorway, was her Uncle Joel, his thin lips quivering as he surveyed the damage.

Janet winced, then tried to explain how it had happened. "You left the door open, Uncle," she finished lamely.

Uncle Joel suddenly relaxed. "My fault, of course," he admitted. "I should have closed it. But I was just going upstairs for a sweater, and it didn't even occur to me. Oh, well."

Janet adored her Uncle Joel. He had taken her in five years ago, after both her parents were killed in an automobile accident. Janet didn't quite understand Uncle Joel or his work, but she knew that he was a biochemist. Each summer, when they came to their woodland cottage in the Adirondacks, he spent his time puttering about in his lab, conducting all sorts of weird experiments.

In his usual good-natured manner, Uncle Joel smiled at Janet and began wiping up the mess on the worktable. "Nothing important," he said. "Just a minor experiment I can easily set up again. Now go out and play with Floppy." He playfully scratched the raccoon under the ear before Janet carried him out of the lab.

Janet wanted to repay her uncle for his kindness. So, during the next three days, she shined his shoes each morning, put his toast on before he came down for breakfast, and washed the dishes after he left for the lab. Uncle Joel was pleased, and this made Janet glow inside.

It was not until the afternoon of the third day that Janet discovered the shocking change in Floppy. When she put out his bowl of raccoon food, he didn't come ambling up to it in his funny hunched-up way; instead, he walked up to it slowly and sedately. Upon peering into his masked-bandit eyes, Janet could have sworn she saw a thoughtful glint there. "Oh, it's just my imagination," she muttered.

"Hungry?" she asked, talking to Floppy as she always did.

"*Hungry*," said the raccoon as he daintily picked up some food with one of his front paws.

"WHAT DID YOU SAY?" gasped Janet. She

25

couldn't believe her ears! "I—I mean—you didn't *really* say anything, did you? Oh, how silly can I be. Animals can't talk."

"*Floppy can talk*," returned the raccoon.

This time, the words were too clear and distinct for Janet to doubt she had heard them. "Floppy!" she cried. "What's happened to you!" When she got no response, she began pointing at nearby objects and giving their names.

"*Rock. Flower. Rake,*" Floppy repeated after her. "*Grass. Bowl. Test tube.*"

The last word made Janet jump up, with Floppy in her arms. "Maybe Uncle Joel can figure out how this happened!"

When Janet first announced that Floppy could talk, Uncle Joel just frowned. "I think you've been reading too much science fiction," he chuckled. But as Janet hurriedly continued her story, explaining how Floppy had licked up the spilled chemicals, her uncle became more and more attentive. Finally, he looked the raccoon in the eyes and began rattling off the names of several objects in his laboratory.

"*Beaker,*" echoed Floppy in a squeaky but distinct voice. "*Chemical. Bunsen burner. Sulfuric acid.*"

Flabbergasted, Uncle Joel slumped into his chair and mopped his brow. "A talking raccoon!" he

murmured. "It's absolutely impossible, and yet . . . "
He looked up at the shelf where all his chemicals
were kept and searched for the missing jar. "Poly-
merase enzyme," he said. "Floppy knocked it off
the shelf, and it mixed with the chemical agents on
my worktable: phospholipid-S21, ribonucleopro-
tein, and vaspressin. Some sheerly accidental com-
pound must have resulted, and—*and Floppy licked
it off his paws*! Yes, that explains everything!"

He grabbed Janet by the shoulders. "Do you know
what this means, child? Your pet raccoon accidentally created a serum that stimulated his brain and
gave him intelligence enough to hear and repeat
human words—and maybe even *think* a little,
unlike a parrot. Why, it's absolutely incredible!"

His face was alight with wonder and excitement.
"This is one of the greatest scientific breakthroughs
of all time!" he shouted. "With the serum, scientists
will be able to make ALL animals talk . . ." A
wry look came into his face. "Just think of it," he
said whimsically, "dogs and cats talking back to
their masters!" But his humorous expression soon
changed, becoming proud and lofty. "When I
demonstrate Floppy's speaking ability to biologists,
they'll go wild. Absolutely wild. It'll stand the
scientific world on its head!"

Janet's face clouded. "Do you mean that Floppy

will be taken away from me?" she asked.

Uncle Joel patted her on the head. "Don't worry, child," he said. "I'll get you another pet. That's a promise."

"But I don't want another pet," said Janet. "I want Floppy! I love him." Janet was on the verge of tears, but her uncle was too busy to notice. He was already making notes of the chemicals involved in the unscheduled "experiment" of three days before.

During the next several days, Janet's uncle spent every waking moment testing out Floppy's newly acquired power of speech. Then he gave the raccoon a battery of IQ tests. Finally, after a week of tests, Uncle Joel revealed his findings to Janet. "Floppy's no genius," he began. "He's just an animal with an activated brain who can carry on basic conversations and absorb simple thoughts. He's far more intelligent than a chimp, however. I'd say he's about halfway between an ape and a man—and believe me, that's saying something! Yes, Janet, there's no doubt about it: when your raccoon knocked over that jar, he created a brain serum that can increase intelligence."

Janet had a vague idea about what such a serum might lead to, but she wasn't sure about it. "Do you mean that the serum might make people—like you and me—twice as smart?" she asked. At her uncle's nod, she asked the crucial question: "Uncle Joel, have you made any more of it?"

Uncle Joel's face fell. "No," he answered, "I'm afraid I haven't. I know what chemicals went into the mixture, but I don't know in what proportions or in what order. I've been trying to reproduce the serum for days now, and I haven't even come close." He pointed to a cage full of rabbits. "See, none of them can even say *boo*."

Early the next morning, Uncle Joel called Janet into his laboratory. "It's about Floppy," he said, propping Janet up on his lap while Floppy sat on the floor licking his fur. "Now, Janet," Uncle Joel continued, "I know you're attached to the little fellow, but you must try to understand my position. You see, there's only *one way* for me to determine the chemical makeup of the serum he produced, and that's—and that's to *extract* it from his bloodstream and vital organs."

Janet jumped off his lap and stared at him in horror. "You mean, Floppy will have to be *killed*?"

Uncle Joel nodded his head.

"NO!" cried Janet. "I won't let you do it! I won't let you kill him!"

"I'm sorry, child," said Uncle Joel, "but I can't let the life of one small animal stand in the way of what will surely be a scientific milestone." His voice became firm and unrelenting. "I'm afraid you'll just have to accept it, Janet. Tomorrow morning, I'm taking Floppy to a biological lab where he'll be put to sleep and—and dissected. It will all be quite painless, I assure you. Now, no more tantrums, Janet."

Janet squeezed back the tears. "Look," she said, pointing to Floppy, "he *heard* you, and he's frightened." Floppy had stopped licking his fur and was staring at Uncle Joel with a stunned look in his eyes.

"Nonsense!" laughed Uncle Joel. "Floppy can't understand life and death and such complicated processes as dissection. He can't possibly know he's going to die."

At Janet's pleading, Floppy's "termination" was delayed for another day. Janet wanted to spend just a little more time with her beloved pet. She hugged Floppy tightly, then broke into tears.

"Janet crying?" asked Floppy, now able to associate ideas to that extent.

"Oh, Floppy," Janet sobbed, "if only the serum would wear off. Then you would stop talking. And with no serum left inside you, Uncle Joel wouldn't have any reason to take you away from me."

Suddenly, Janet's face lit up. "Why not?" she whispered. "If I *tell* Floppy to stop talking and play dumb, Uncle Joel will be fooled!" The joyous glint in her eyes soon faded away. "No," she moaned, "I can't do that. If I did, I'd be robbing Uncle Joel of all his big plans, and I'd be holding back science. But I can't sit back and let Floppy die! Oh, what am I going to do?"

Janet turned to stroke the raccoon's fur. "Good thing you can't understand big thoughts," she said, "or you'd be just as confused as I am. Come on, Floppy, let's go back to the house and get something to eat."

She started to walk away, then turned. "Come on, Floppy!" she yelled. "You heard me." In the past few days, Floppy had understood and responded to her every word; but now, he ignored her and rolled in the grass as any ordinary pet might do.

A glimmer of hope stirred within Janet. "Floppy," she said, "what's my name? Come on, say it." Saying nothing, the raccoon looked up and gave her a vacant stare.

Janet still wasn't satisfied; she needed more proof. Frantically, she began pointing to things and demanding that Floppy name them. But all her attempts to make him talk failed. Floppy said nothing.

"Oh, Floppy!" She picked him up and hugged him happily. "The miracle I prayed for has happened! *You're dumb again*! I'm sorry for Uncle

31

Joel, but I'm happy for you—and me."

Janet dropped Floppy to the ground, raced toward the house, and ran down the stairs to her uncle's laboratory. She could hardly wait to tell Uncle Joel the wonderful news: the brain serum had *worn off*, leaving Floppy just an ordinary raccoon and not a phenomenal talking animal.

"NOT TALKING ANY MORE!" responded her uncle in a shrill voice. "Why, that ruins everything! Are you sure about this, child?"

"Yes!" Janet replied. "I'll bring him here so you can see for yourself."

As Janet approached Floppy from behind, she thought she heard him muttering something to himself. She wasn't sure, but it sounded like he was saying: *"No more talking. No more talking, or Floppy will die. . . ."*

Startled, Janet stopped in her tracks. "Surely he can't be THAT smart," she thought. And yet, the muffled noises he was making sounded a lot like words to her.

Vaguely, Janet remembered something she had learned in school, in animal studies. Her teacher had been talking about instincts, and she had said that there was one instinct that was stronger than any other—in every living creature. And that was the instinct of *self-preservation.*

The
Good Old
Days

It started off as just another ordinary day. John and George were arguing again while Waldo, the family robot, was serving them a breakfast of vitameal and reconstituted milk.

"I don't care what you say. Nothing's fun any more," said John. "It's a boring summer. There's nothing to do but the same old stuff." Waldo asked him if he wanted more milk, but John put his palm over the top of his glass.

"What are you talking about?" asked George. "We had a good time yesterday, at Rockefeller Center."

"You mean swimming in that dumb oxygen pool? Big deal, you can breathe under water. I'm sick of doing that. I'd rather be living in the twentieth century. Then, they had cars you could duck in front of, and games like stickball and kick-the-can, and everything was dangerous. People really had a good time back then."

"Do you remember how an oxy-pool works?" asked Waldo, as he poured more milk into John's glass.

"Oh, no, here he goes again," George said.

"Yes, yes, I know," John answered. "Oxygen is forced into the water under pressure."

"It may seem simple to you, but it took people a long time to realize that it wasn't the water that drowns you, but the lack of oxygen." Obviously proud of himself, Waldo rolled out of the dining room into the kitchen, only to return with two saucers filled with imitation fruit.

"See," said John, "the fruit's not even real! In the olden days, they used to have *real* fruit."

"We still have some real fruit left," said Waldo in a somewhat metallic voice. "We just have to ration it. But no one is starving any more, and there are almost 9 billion people on this planet."

"Yeah," said John, "but in the twentieth century, there were a lot less people, and a lot more room to have fun. Lots of open spaces and deserts and stuff."

"But millions of people were starving and suffering from disease," said Waldo.

"Phooey," said John. "At least the world wasn't boring then."

John continued to find the world boring for the rest of the morning and afternoon. George had gone to his room to study—his pre-engineering boards were coming up—so John took an air-train to Long Island Sound to go dolphin riding. But he wasn't really in the mood to meet his dolphin friends, and he returned after an hour of splashing in the green, unpolluted swim area.

"Hello, is anybody home?" John shouted as the door slid shut behind him. He walked through the apartment, checking the rooms. "Wonder where Waldo is?" he thought. "Must be with George."

George's room was at the end of the hall. But George wasn't there. And neither was Waldo. Something was wrong with the room; it was filled with a golden haze, and large numbers and letters were blinking on and off over a small black box on the night stand.

"Oh, no!" John gasped. He knew what the black box was: it was a *time machine*, the smallest and most advanced kind in the world. But how did it get here? You needed a special permit to use one of those things.

The machine had been turned on, and that spelled trouble. George and Waldo had apparently used it. Now, they were somewhere in another time. But where? John read the numbers and code letters. They said: Y-E-A-R 1-9-7-3. R-E-A-D-Y A-C-T-I-V-A-T-E.

The machine hummed louder as John approached it. He was scared, but he had to find his brother and Waldo; they were probably in trouble. Suddenly, John felt the room begin to spin. He was falling, falling into an endless well. Silver dots swirled behind his eyelids, and he heard noises and shouts all around him.

"Who are you?" someone asked. When John opened his eyes, he saw a girl with short black hair and round eyeglasses standing over him. She wore a striped overgarment and blue pantaloons. John remembered that the pantaloons were called "jeans." Horns blared and people shouted in the street. The air smelled bad. John coughed.

"Holy cow!" shouted the girl. "You just popped out of nowhere—just like that. Poof! Boy, I never thought anything like this would ever happen to me. *Nothing* ever happens to me. Until just now, this has been a really boring summer."

"I'm from the future," John said. "The rest is too complicated to explain. But I've got to find my brother, George, and our family robot, Waldo."

"Waldo?" asked the girl. "Is he a real robot?"

"Yes, I just told you that. Now will you help me look for my brother? I don't know my way around here." John looked around at the cement buildings that rose into the sky. And he felt the thrill of danger as the cars whisked past him, close enough for him to touch.

"Sure. I'll help you find them," said the girl. "My name's Pam. What's yours?"

"John."

"Boy, what a break," Pam said. "What a lousy summer this has been—nothing but stickball and kick-the-can all day. Most of the kids have left the city with their parents for vacations, and the air has been really bad all summer long. Lately, I've been staying home and reading comics."

"That sounds like fun," John said.

"Naw, even comics get boring after a while. Same old thing."

"What's all the shouting about down the street?" John asked.

"I don't know, probably a robbery or something."

"Well, I'm going to find out," John said. As he ran down the street, horrible thoughts flashed through his mind: perhaps his brother was there, and someone was hurting him.

"Watch out for the cars!" Pam yelled.

John could see the crowd at the end of the street. Forgetting about Pam, he pushed his way in. And there was Waldo, backed against a brick wall, his house-cleaning extenders waving above his round metal head. People were throwing rocks and garbage at him.

"Over here, Waldo!" shouted John.

As Waldo rolled toward John, the crowd suddenly started yawning. Soon, they fell asleep right on the street, all happily sighing and snoring.

"They will sleep for just a few minutes," Waldo said, pulling John and Pam toward him with his extenders. "I'm only equipped to defend. I cannot harm anyone."

John wanted to tell Waldo how happy he was to see him, but he couldn't say anything except, "Where's George?"

"I don't know," answered Waldo. "But we can't get back without him, because he has the control unit to the time machine."

"Wow, you're really a robot, just like in the movies," Pam said. "Why didn't you use your sleep ray on the crowd before?"

"It's not a 'sleep ray,' as you call it, young lady. And the reason I didn't use it earlier was that I wanted to draw attention to myself so that George might find me. As it turned out, John found me instead. Now we're *all* in trouble, so we'd better find George."

"If we find your brother, can I go into the future with you?" Pam asked John. "We could have lots of fun there with all the robots and time machines and neat things like that. I bet you have a lot more fun than we do."

"We'd better leave this place quickly," interrupted Waldo. "Those people will be waking up very soon."

So they left the neighborhood and found an alley to hide in. John looked up and wondered why the sky was so gray and smoky. He had forgotten that motors were very crude in the twentieth century, polluting the air and making people sick.

"We can't look for your brother with Waldo along," Pam said, "unless you want to put the whole city to sleep. But if he could pull in his arms and those wiggly things, he might just pass as a modern statue until we find your brother."

And that's exactly what they did. While Waldo stood on Fifty-second Street, pretending to be a statue, Pam and John combed the neighborhood for George.

"I'm getting tired," said Pam. "We'd better find him soon, because I'm supposed to be home for dinner."

"But I thought you wanted to come with us," John said.

"I don't know," Pam said. "Maybe I should stay here, after all. The twentieth century doesn't have robots and time machines, but it has my family and friends, and I know my way around here. Maybe I could come for a visit sometime."

John wished that he was back home with Waldo and George, like before. Right now, the future looked good, even if it wasn't exciting. And perhaps it was more exciting than he'd given it credit for. After all this smoke and smog, a dip in the oxy-pool would be a treat. And if he stayed here, he could never ride the dolphins again, and never see his parents. And this was such a dirty place.

"There he is!" shouted John. "Hey, George! Wait!"

George had just stepped out of a museum. "What are YOU doing here?" he asked John.

"You didn't shut the time machine off," John explained, "and Waldo came looking for you. And I thought you were both in trouble."

"Boy, am I going to be in trouble *now*!" George exclaimed. "How could I have forgotten to turn the time machine off?"

"How did you get the machine, anyway?" John asked.

"It was sent to our address by mistake. And since it was there, I thought I'd try it out. Where's Waldo?"

"Waiting for us. Do you have the control unit?"

George took the silver box from his pocket and gave it to John. "Did you have a good time?"

"Well, I met Pam," John said. "But I don't want to stay here. This is a nice place to visit, but it doesn't have robots and oxy-pools and dolphins. And you have to get back and study for your exams."

"Okay, let's get Waldo," said George . . .

. . . "Goodbye, Pam," said John.

"Maybe we can get permission to visit again and bring you back for a while," George said.

Waldo looked very nervous. Finally, John pushed the button on the control unit, and they left the twentieth century. John had no regrets about returning to his own time. "It's good to be home again," he thought.

Later that day, after they had delivered the time machine to the proper address, John and George went to Rockefeller Center and took a dip in the oxy-pool. Waldo, of course, was waiting for them when they returned home.

"Even if the present *is* a little boring," thought John, "there's always the *future* to explore!"

Laurence M. Janifer

Story
Time

Gerald Orson Willis told stories. He never wrote them down because he owned a very fine tape recorder. He told his stories to the tape recorder, and someone else took the tapes and put the stories into books like this one. You probably know some of them.

But you don't know *this* one; Gerald Orson Willis never told it. I'm telling it, because it's important. And I'm not using his tape recorder, either . . .

. . . You see, Gerald Orson Willis's tape recorder was the only one of its kind. Because of a very special mistake in the tape-recorder factory—a mistake involving five different parts—it recorded *true* stores. In other words, everything that was said into the tape recorder came true.

At first, Gerald Orson Willis didn't know that his tape recorder was so special, because most of his stories were about the future. But one day, he turned on the tape recorder and began telling a story about his own time. The story went exactly like this:

On July 15, 1973, a Martian named Xixobrax came to Earth and began to study it. He wanted to conquer Earth, but he couldn't figure out how. So the Martian decided to ask an Earth person for some help.

The story never got any further than that, because there was a knock at the door, and Gerald Orson Willis had to get up and answer it. When he opened the door, his eyes almost popped out of his head. He couldn't say anything for a while, or even move. This was only natural, because Gerald Orson Willis had never seen a real, live Martian before—especially not a Martian named Xixobrax!

The Martian clicked its claws at him and said, "Hello."

After a long time, Gerald finally said, "Hello," too. He couldn't think of anything else to say. The Martian was bright green, and over eight feet tall, with 12 brown eyes running down his body like coat buttons. The sight of all those eyes made Gerald very nervous.

"I don't know how to conquer Earth," the Martian said.

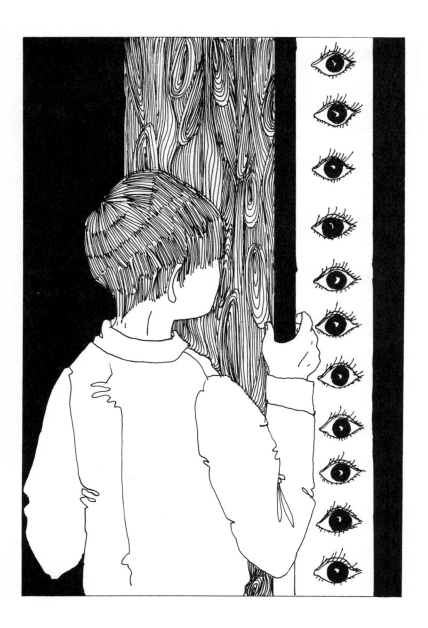

Gerald tried to breathe evenly. "That's too bad," he said.

"You have to help me," the Martian said.

"Why?" Gerald asked, thinking that he already knew the answer.

He was right. "Because you made me up," the Martian said. "And because you made me want to conquer the world. I'm really a peaceful sort of Martian, but you made me want to conquer Earth. And now, you have to tell me how." His eyes blinked on and off, one at a time, bottom to top.

Gerald Orson Willis was more nervous now than before. He thought that a Martian conquering the world was a good story, but not so good in real life. So, when he could breathe evenly again, he asked, "What will happen to me if I don't help you?"

"Not much," the Martian said. "Except I'll stay here, for as long as it takes. I don't think you'd like that. I'm peaceful, but I get hungry — and one of the things I like eating most is human beings!"

Gerald sat down on the floor and tried to think. He had dreamed up the Martian for his story, and the Martian had come true. This meant that there was something very special about him — the writer — or about his *tape recorder*. To solve the mystery, he turned the tape recorder on. "Xixobrax was holding a candy cane in one claw," he said, and all at once, a candy cane appeared in the Martian's right claw! Then Gerald turned the tape recorder off. "In the other claw, the Martian was holding a bunch of flowers," he said. But nothing happened this time. No flowers—nothing.

The Martian was looking at the candy cane, wondering if it was something to eat or a new secret weapon. All he had to do to conquer Earth was to say, "Xixobrax conquered Earth," while the tape recorder was still on. But he didn't know that yet. Besides, he was too busy trying to figure out the candy cane.

Gerald thought of telling the tape recorder that Xixobrax didn't exist any more. But that would be too much like killing, he decided. So instead, he asked the Martian, "Except for conquering Earth, what do you really want?"

Xixobrax's eyes blinked on and off again, one at a time. (Martians do that when they think really hard.) "I'd like to go back to Mars," he said at last. "It's more comfortable there. And I'd like to take some of these things with me." He waved the candy cane in the air. "I think I can eat them. I get hungry a lot—and once I'm back on Mars, I won't be able to eat people any more."

"Oh," Gerald said. Then, before the Martian could figure out the secret of the tape recorder, he turned the machine on and said, "Xixobrax went back to Mars, carrying 600 candy canes." To his relief, it worked. Covered by brand-new candy canes, the Martian disappeared.

Gerald took a deep breath. Then he stood up and stared at the tape recorder, knowing that anything he said into it would come true. He thought about money, and fame, and gold, and candy canes. But he finally decided that he had done enough harm with the tape recorder. If he made anything else come true, he might do even more harm, and he might have a much harder time fixing it up.

So Gerald Orson Willis did a very hard thing: he sold the tape recorder, and bought a new one. A normal one . . .

. . . You probably think that Gerald Orson Willis did the right thing. But you're wrong! He should have burned the tape recorder, or at least have told it not to go on making things come true. Because that tape recorder *still exists*, somewhere. And anything anyone says near it, while it's on, is going to come true!

I don't know where it is any more.

That's why I'm telling you this story.

Please, be careful about what you say—

The tape recorder might be listening!

The Lerner Science Fiction Library

Night of the Sphinx and Other Stories

Adrift in Space and Other Stories

The Killer Plants and Other Stories

The Tunnel and Other Stories

Journey to Another Star and Other Stories

The Missing World and Other Stories

The Graduated Robot and Other Stories

The Mind Angel and Other Stories

We specialize in publishing quality books for young people. For a complete list please write:

LERNER PUBLICATIONS COMPANY

241 First Avenue North, Minneapolis, Minnesota 55401